COME HERE, CLEO!

Caroline Mockford

Barefoot Books
better books for children

Cleo wakes.

Cleo winks.

Cleo yawns.

Cleo blinks.

Cleo wants to play.

Cleo jumps outside.

Cleo tries
to climb.

Cleo
slips
and
slides.

Cleo sees a tree.

Cleo skips and hops.

Cleo meets a bird.

Cleo wobbles...

Cleo drops.

Cleo bounces.

Cleo chases.

Cleo pounces.

Cleo dashes.

Cleo misses.

"Come here, Cleo!"

Cleo kisses.

For Kit — C. M.
For Zoë — S. B.

Barefoot Books, Inc.
37 West 17th St
4th Floor East
New York, New York 10011

The illustrations were prepared in acrylics on 140lb watercolor paper

Graphic design by Jennie Hoare, England
This book was typeset in 44pt Providence Sans Bold
Color separation by Bright Arts Graphics, Singapore
Printed and bound in Singapore by Tien Wah Press (Pte) Ltd

This book has been printed on 100% acid-free paper

1 3 5 7 9 8 6 4 2

U.S. Cataloging-in-Publication Data
(Library of Congress Standards)

Mockford, Caroline.
    Come Here, Cleo! / Caroline Mockford [ill.] ; [text
by Stella Blackstone]- Colophon. — 1st ed.
[24] p. : col. ill. ;   cm.
Summary: The story of a small cat's playful adventures
as she investigates the world outdoors.
ISBN 1-84148-329-X
1. Cats—Fiction. I. Blackstone, Stella. II. Title.
[E] 21 2001   AC   CIP